My Dog Jack Is FAT

by
Eve Bunting

illustrated by
Michael Rex

Marshall Cavendish Children

Text copyright © 2011 by Eve Bunting

Illustrations copyright © 2011 by Michael Rex

Marshall Cavendish Corporation, 99 White Plains Road, Tarrytown, NY 10591

www.marshallcavendish.us/kids

Library of Congress Cataloging-in-Publication Data

Bunting, Eve, 1928-

My dog Jack is fat / by Eve Bunting ; illustrated by Michael Rex. — 1st

ed.

p. cm.

Summary: Carson does his best to help his dog, Jack, lose weight, with

unexpected results.

ISBN 978-0-7614-5809-8

[1. Weight control—Fiction. 2. Dogs—Fiction.] I. Rex, Michael, ill. II.

Title.

PZ7.B91527Myd 2011

[E]—dc22

2010018271

The illustrations are rendered in colored pencil, with color added digitally.

Book design by Anahid Hamparian

Editor: Margery Cuyler

Printed in China (E)

First edition

1 3 5 6 4 2

Marshall Cavendish Children

To Keelin Taylor Bunting, with love
—E.B.

To Pepper and Casey
—M.R.

One day, Carson took Jack to the vet.

It was hungry work watching Jack exercise.

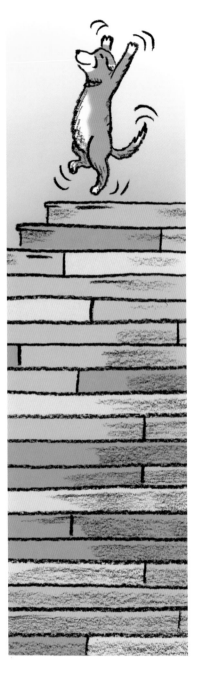

Every day, Carson took Jack to the gym.

Carson took Jack to the beach.
Carson slept on his beach towel,
while Jack had lots of fun.

Finally, the month was up. It was time to go back to the vet.

When Carson and Jack got home, they stood in front of the mirror.